ALL THE BROKEN PIECES

VOLUME 1

H. M. WARD

LAREE BAILEY PRESS

LAREE BAILEY PRESS

First Edition: November 2019

ISBN: 978-1-63035-240-0 (Paperback)

ISBN: 978-1-63035-239-4

TERMS & SLANG USED IN ALL IN THE BROKEN PIECES SERIES

*E*ver wonder what the heck an idiom means? Never heard a slang term before?

Below is a list of the most commonly used verbiage in this series and the meaning in plain English.

Asshat (v): Demeanor and actions that are unattractively dickish.

Awesomesauce *(adj.)*: A way to describe something that is beyond awesome with a dash of excitement. Typically said by women.

Name-ism *(n)*: Typically two common turns-of-phrase that were mashed together to create a new, more pungent meaning.

Babylon *(n):* A township on Long Island where Avery grew up. There are million-dollar homes on the waterfront to tiny Cape Cod houses.

Cleavagefest *(adv):* When a woman's breasts are thrust up and smashed together so tightly that it infers a sexy party may be imminent.

Cray Cray *(adj):* Super, over-the-top crazy.

Deer Park Avenue *(n):* A heavily congested road that runs through several towns on Long Island.

Guido *(n):* An Italian young man.

Guidette *(n):* An Italian young woman.

L.I.E. *(n):* The Long Island Expressway, or Interstate 495, is a six-lane road the runs East/ West on Long Island that ends in Manhattan.

Skankzilla (adj): A woman who is part godzilla and part skank.

Slutified (v): When the amount of skin a piece of clothing covers is severely decreased to reveal more skin.

Squee *(v):* A squeal of glee. Try it. You'll like it.

Tramperella (adj): A promiscuous woman who has access to Cinderella's royal closet and slutified the garments.

*H*ey Ferro fans! I'm looking for a few die-hard Ferro fans to be on my ELITE STREET TEAM.

Qualifications: You need to:

1. ♡ the Ferro family.

2. Have a favorite Ferro who you know everything about.

3. Read all the Ferro books.

4. Consider yourself a Ferro expert.

5. Be willing & ready to take action—that could be anything from posting a review of a new title on Goodreads, to spearheading a Ferro fun night on FB, to leading the Netflix push for our movie, to ushering at a live Ferro event. Basically, you can't shut up about the Ferro family and would squee with glee to be involved in official HM Ward activities (online and/ or off).

I just can't do everything by myself. It's a lot. And honestly, you guys are amazing and fun. A small crew of die-hard, I-know-every-thing-Ferro folks is just what we need!

Those involved get access to Beta reading, ARCs, signed books, events, backstage access, HM Ward swag, and more!

If you're interested, read on. ☺ If you can't do everything but would be the best blogger we ever had, dude! Come sign up.

Tasks will be sorted based on who can do what. In other words, you don't have to be able to be everywhere all the time—even though you want to. Make sense?

Who wants in? Come over to Club Ferro to request an application.

SUGGESTED FERRO READING
ORDER

EACH SERIES CAN BE READ
INDIVIDUALLY OR YOU CAN
FOLLOW THE PUBLICATION
ORDER BELOW.

THE ARRANGEMENT 1
  THE ARRANGEMENT 2
THE ARRANGEMENT 3
THE ARRANGEMENT 4
THE ARRANGEMENT 5
THE ARRANGEMENT 6
DAMAGED 1
DAMAGED 2
SECRET LIFE OF TRYSTAN SCOTT 1
SECRET LIFE OF TRYSTAN SCOTT 2
SECRET LIFE OF TRYSTAN SCOTT 3
SECRET LIFE OF TRYSTAN SCOTT 4
SECRET LIFE OF TRYSTAN SCOTT 5
THE ARRANGEMENT 7
THE ARRANGEMENT 8

To all those with a broken heart and endless hope.
Hang in there...

ALL THE BROKEN PIECES

VOLUME 1

READ ME, BABE!

*T*hank you to everyone who supported this project! Before you start, a quick heads-up.

THIS SERIES IS FAN-DRIVEN. So I'll release a new novella when enough people ask for another book via reviews and social media. When tons of people ask and are involved, the next book comes out <u>fast</u>.

So if you like the idea and love the book, make sure you do both! Having that bit of reader involvement makes a huge difference in the success of a series. It'll also make sure you don't miss any voting that occurs as the series progresses.

Last thing—there are **'Easter eggs' in this**

book. One per chapter. An 'Easter egg' in this case is a hidden bit from one of my other books. It can be anything from DEMON KISSED to DAMAGED 3.

An example would be seeing a Trystan Scott poster or passing by Ivy's high school in Demon Kissed. This is a fun game for those who have read all my books. If this is your first book of mine or you haven't read every-thing, it doesn't affect the way the book reads at all. It's just fun hidden surprises. I did this on a smaller scale with SCANDALOUS and STRIPPED. Have fun with it! ☺

This series has been three years in the making. It's tense, raw, and dark. I almost didn't publish it, but you guys cheered me on, so here it is. Thank you so much! Happy reading!

You can join in the discussion via my Facebook page: www. facebook.com/AuthorHMWard.

For a complete listing of Ferro books, look here: http://hmward.com/books/

Thank you and happy reading!

~Holly

CHAPTER 1

*H*overing over my gradebook, I lean hard with both elbows on the countertop and thread my fingers through my hair. The cotton balls that were contained to my throat have manage to claw their way into my mouth. My lips feel like they were doused with sand. The little black brick of a computer sits in front of me, between my elbows. Case closed. Normally, I wouldn't care so much. I wouldn't feel this lasso around my neck tightening as the clock on the wall ticks down the minutes until the bell rings and students fill the hallways.

Dread bloats within me, leaving a rancid taste in my mouth. If my stomach wasn't tied like a right knot maybe I could think. Or breathe. This part never gets easier. It doesn't matter how many months pass or how much interest I take in work. It doesn't matter how much I sleep. How much I exercise. How much I drink. How much I regret. How much I forgive. Nothing helps.

Sighing deeply, I glance at the classroom. The afternoon sun floods through the window slicing the art room in half. Half desks and chairs, half cabinets filled with supplies, sinks, and student's artwork. Some of the cabinets are mine. Budget cuts. I don't know a single teacher who hasn't supplemented their class budget with their own money. It's just the way it is here.

The gray silk blouse I donned this morning to keep me cool clings to my body like wet toilet paper. Sweat drips between my breasts and down the small of my back where it's sponged up by my pants. My hair is twisted up on top of my head and stabbed with a 6B pencil. Despite holding the tresses off my neck, it's still slick with sweat. A few wayward strands curl tightly, hovering just above my damp skin. Thank God this isn't a freshman class, or it'd be full of bodies making the room warmer. It's the end of the school year and the heat is overly oppressive. Since my school district isn't loaded, there's no AC. Not even in the teacher's lounge.

On any given day, with the heat index at 98 and hundreds of bodies trapped inside a cinderblock building, it could be the reason why I feel this way—lethargic and frantic to the point that I could be sick at any moment. A ripple moves from the clavicle at the base of my throat up towards my mouth. My skin is covered in tingles and I shiver. Hesitating. I have a few moments. I rest my palms on the laptop, lid shut.

Glancing around, I admire my students. Their diligence. Determination. Two things I once possessed. Two things completely foreign to me now. There was a time when I was passionate about art, love, and life. Those embers died. Maybe petrified and turned to stone.

The kids worked hard this year. I see their potential even if mine was washed away. If I had it to do all over again, I'd probably make the same mistakes. I relive that damn day every hour, but on days like this when the temperature is high, my tolerance to keep the memories at bay is low. If I catch the scent of lilies there's no way to stop the torrent of memories that appear so vividly that it feels like I'm there, reliving that horror. My mind won't stay on track and it won't until I get this done with. Open the laptop and do it. I breathe in. Exhale.

My eyes water as my gaze fixates on the students, clustered together at the far end of the room, drawing pads on the sill, and pencils in their hands. They are all off to one side trying to sit in a splotch of cool shadow. They talk about the beach, summer plans, and unrealized hopes that pop up like spring daisies. Guard your heart. I want to warn them, but I haven't a clue how to do it. I've been living on autopilot for years, waiting for my motherboard to fry or come back online.

Remember the first version of AOL where you'd sit there listening to the screech of the modem while waiting for something to happen? To connect or get rejected. By a fictional blue man trying to outrun a triangle. Needless to say, I don't relate to normal things anymore. The truth is, I'm a horrible person. I did something hideous. It'd be different if I couldn't live with myself and cried my eyes out, but I don't cry. Sand. My head, eyes, throat, and mouth are constantly cotton-balled. Maybe I have no soul. I don't think I'm a sociopath, but how would I know? It's not like people raise their hands to get tested for that sort of thing.

My eyes shift to the side again as I throw my gaze onto my laptop. At some point, I straightened my back and started wringing my hands. They're slick. My fingertips have turned white. Damn. Just do it. Stop being such an ass. What's the worst thing that could happen?

Pictures. Photos can't hurt me.

Just get it over with. I shift my weight, perched on a tall stool, leaving one of my ballet flats on the floor with the other hooked over the lowest rim of the footrest. Pressing my cracked lips together, I smooth my shirt. There's a V of sweat down the front of my once pristine blouse. The idea was to dress retro. Not the way kids do, but with a classic Audrey Hepburn look. Dark hair pulled back, slim capris nearly to the ankle, ballet shoe, topped off with a silk blouse with a sash at the waist. It looked amazing when it wasn't soaking with sweat.

The plastic of the computer case feels cold to the touch. I slip my index finger under the rim and flip open the lid. The screen lights up and a web browser opens. I type in the letters. Pull up the website. Facebook. Every forty-year-old woman's dream. A stream of consciousness from the past and the present colliding in one place, coupled with ads, haters, over-sharers, trolls, and fake news. Years ago, it was fun. Now? Not so much. But everything was exciting once. The memories of me laughing so hard it hurt have faded to nothing. I don't remember what it feels like to smile anymore. The tightness of my mouth hints at a severe issue with RBF (resting bitch face). I've been called worse.

Why am I sporting the social media alba-tross? Somehow communicating with parents via social media has become normal —expected. For normal people it's not a problem. I mean, think about it. Facebook is the social media equivalent of a labradoodle on pixie sticks. It's excited to see you. So much so that it licks you with memories, photos, and ads of everything, all at once, tail wagging, eyes wide with no regard for your past. For the pain. It's a robodog. How could it possibly know I'd rather shove this pencil through my eye than log into my account? It doesn't know because normal people like to see all this stuff.

I'm not normal. I don't want to see it. But I've learned to take the hits life throws my way. I get knocked on my ass, lose a few years of my life, and get back up. When I was younger, I thought bouncing back meant full mental and emotional recovery. Ready to grin again—laugh life in the face and say, *'you can't get me.'*

The truth is no one recovers. Every human over the age of twenty-nine is a patchwork of pain, suffering, and antidepressants.

CHAPTER 2

*T*he concept of cheer flew away and all comprehension of what joy felt like is now a shadow. But we press on because what else would we do? Waste hundreds of hours on social media, crying out into the vastness, hoping for an echo of peace that never comes? Nah, not me. I only login to this beast when absolutely necessary.

Brace for impact. My teeth tap together as my jaw clenches. The little muscle at the bottom, back by my ear, twitches. The page loads and I'm in. Facebook blasts me with pictures from my past. I see them before I can click away to post the message for the student art show on the school's event page.

Clicking away is hard when I've packed up every part of this old life. I haven't looked at these old pictures since last term when I logged on to post the Winter Art show for the school. And I fall for it every time. The barrage of images. I have to visually drink in everything I lost. It's like passing by a car wreck without looking. So, I look.

There, at the top of my newsfeed is Zach's beautiful smiling face—that angular jaw dusted in dark stubble with piercing blue eyes. Those lips tipped up in one corner with a boyish smile that promises everything. Memories not posted on any website flash behind my eyes. His voice. His lips on my neck, the heat of his kiss on my skin as our bodies tangled together. The way he yelled. How nastily we fought.

It happens so fast. One picture conjures so many memories and a myriad of emotions. But that life is gone. I flip past it, bracing myself and chasing away the remnant phantom feelings caressing my skin. Love and hate mingle—they feel nearly identical.

As I scroll down the page to get to the

spot where I can click off into the school's parents' group, my newsfeed wags its tail trying to get my attention. It fills with pissed off people raging against the ending of their favorite TV series, then a bottle blonde telling me I should get her amazing leg make-up, and sure-fire diet ads. But then the bitch gets personal.

REMEMBER WHEN? The two words I avoid at all cost are plastered on my screen.

The words pop up, showcasing a picture from long ago of me and Zara in a boat at Belmont Lake. Best-friends, standing together with my arm draped over her shoulders. We stand on the shore before the docks, with the boathouse behind us. A gaggle of psycho-geese inch their way closer to where we were standing. Her dark eyes look out at me as if she were still here. As if she were just around the corner, in the classroom down the hall, where she should be.

The sweat rolling down my back increases. It has nothing to do with the weather. Anger is flickering to life.

Guilt.

Grief.

Fuck. Type faster. A shiver runs over my skin and before I can click away, I find myself staring at her oval face and olive skin. No one could do make-up like Zara. She made it look so effortless. Echoes of her laughter fill my mind, the scent of warm vanilla emanates from nowhere. The memory conjures so vividly that I can hear the faint echoes of her voice. Smell that perfume that she wore every day. Even though she's not here anymore.

Scolding myself, I strengthen my resolve and press my palm to my forearm, and smooth the slick, pebbled skin. Erasing the ghosts. There's a point where memories become so real, so inexplicably tangible, that it's as if those horrible events never happened. But they did. In rapid succession my life ended because the two people who consumed it were suddenly gone.

If Zara lived, maybe there'd be a wisp of my former self left. A tiny ribbon, stretched thin, and threadbare—but she'd anchor me. Pull me back.

Zach is another story. He's the reason I

can't remember to breathe. Everything
between us was burned to the ground.
Passion has two sides. Love and hate. I
couldn't make our marriage work anymore.
It turned to cinders in my hands. I didn't
know why he became what he was. Why he
drank himself to oblivion. Why I let him. I
thought he'd right himself and we'd rebound.
But after Zara died, there was no rebound for
either of us. He lost his twin sister and I lost
my best friend.

I didn't think it could get worse, but it
did. We fought. I didn't hold back. I said
words that cut deeply, trying to make him
feel something—react somehow. Until one
day I realized that I believed what I was
saying. Zach and I were done. Anyone could
see it. His mother told me weekly.

When she was nice, she'd say stuff like, "If
you hold onto something so precious too
tightly for too long, you'll smother it."

On a bad day, which was most days for
her, she'd come in sharper, not holding back.
Blame and anger painted every word she
uttered. There was a time when I was
welcome at her house. A time when I was

loved. Not now. I reek of death, she says. It doesn't keep me away. When Zach's brother is out of town, I check in on her—despite her protests. She's a battleax, all brute force when it comes to her mouth, but frailness and age have taken their toll on her body. I have no soul. What she says is almost true, minus some of the racial slurs, so it doesn't bother me. Besides, she's the only mother I've had for over twenty-five years. We're family, like it or not.

This is my life now. Impossibly fake. And terrifyingly real. An invisible hand holds my barely beating heart in its frozen grip, while I plaster a plastic smile on my lips. Faking, pretending my way through the rest of my life. Because I have no clue how to move forward and I can't go back.

My fingers hoover over the keys of the laptop, ready to strike. Facebook is a grave-yard where the dead still live. The family didn't want to delete their pages after their passing, which is understandable. Albeit painful for me. I'd never visit this site again if I had my way. But that's not the way the world works. So, Facebook pops Zach up in my feed as if nothing happened. As if he were alive and we were still in love. As if he's still alive and breathing. As if I didn't tell him I hated him. As if those weren't my final words to the man I loved for twenty years of my life.

The weight in the center of my chest is close to collapsing in on itself. A blackhole will take the place of my heart. I wish I was numb. That I didn't care. But there are things I never should have said to him. And confessions I should have made with Zara. But it's especially hard with Zach. We were so broken by the time we got to that day. The promise of more time was a lie. I thought we had more time to fix things. More time to make up. More time to laugh and move on with our lives. Separate or together, but there would be more time with him. Turns out that wasn't true. Time is a thief and I was robbed blind.

If only one of them died, then I could have handled things better. But losing both? Within twelve months? It was too much. I didn't realize I had a soul until it tore in half.

Now, I walk amongst the living but I'm dead inside. Hollowed out. I've figured out how to function this way. Don't feel sorry for me. I envy the people who thrive living like this. They can make snap decisions without the emotional hangover that follows me like a stray cat. Always there, begging, jumping out of the shadows when least expected.

CHAPTER 3

*Z*ara died first. She passed away about a year before Zach. His twin. I met him because of her. A hint of a smile tugs at my lips but I force it down. Lock it away. She was my college roommate. My best friend. He was her devastatingly beautiful brother. Now they're both ashes.

My throat has turned to chalk. I crack my knuckles and glance around the room. The students are perched on stools at slanted desks with their pencils and drawing pads. They murmur amongst themselves ignoring me, all except Eric who seems preoccupied with some teenage drama. The rest are engrossed in their art or secretly thumbing through their phone screens, thinking I don't see. It's the end of the year. If they turned everything in, I don't 'see' a thing. And neither do they. I'm a widow. The childish rumors say I killed my husband on vacation and buried him at the bottom of the ocean.

I wish I never saw his body. But I did. That memory will haunt me until I take my last breath.

Facebook. Focus. I need to make the post before the bell rings. Before my peers wander in and notice my sweat and pallor has nothing to do with the weather. My finger hoovers over the mouse ready to click away from my feed, but those pictures.... I'm a junkie, wanting a hit—to see a picture of him. Just one more even though it'll end with my heart in pieces and my cheeks covered in tears.

Regrets surges through me. I hate the way things ended with us. I feel like an angry ghost. Robbed of what could have been. We were on the brink of disaster, divorce imminent. Or we were on the precipice of something new. I'll never know. That last fight was left unfinished. Unresolved.

It leaves me feeling agitated because I'm stuck walking a fence for the rest of my life. Was he going to leave me? I never thought we'd fall apart. No one did. It was the type of thing that started the size of a grain of sand. It got in there and grew, festered. Too many things unsaid and too many tears avoided. When we laughed, we laughed. But toward the end, when we fought, it was ugly. I didn't recognize him anymore. At the time I blamed him, and still do—to some extent—but I wasn't me anymore either. I became this placating version of me. Docile, whining, and filterless. I said everything I thought, good and bad. Most of it complaining. Yet, I linger here hoping to see an old picture of him because there are none at home. The past was erased, every photo of us destroyed. So, I perch on this stool, shoulders forward, wringing my fingers hoping for a glimpse of him. Like when we first met.

My stomach sinks and I straighten in my seat. I want to click away. I want to leave the page, but I can't. Instead, I click on private message with a blue dot indicating that it's new. When the screen loads, my face falls when I see who it's from. That little blue dot is perched directly next to Zach's face. It's a message from him. And that blue dot means it's unread.

The way my heart slams into my chest physically aches. This has happened before, the new PM with the blue dot. More than once. Both times it was a glitch. Cruel technological fails. The steel cage I built around my heart—the same cage that saved me and let my soul wither—cracks. In that split-second hope fills my body and my grief falls away. Forgotten. I slap the key, clicking the private message, only to realize it is old. The note was written before he died.

Let's try to work things out. Me & you in the Caymans. Just us. No distractions. What do you say?

The steel cage around my heart fractures. The crevice deepens and I swear I can hear metal torquing. Eyes shining, I want to scream, but I swallow it and manage to keep that plastic smile on my face. I will not break. There is no one to piece me back together if I do...

CHAPTER 4

I stiffen in my seat as a student nears my desk at the front of the classroom. Large windows frame the young woman. She's my little prodigy, Aleigha Thamas. Her dark eyes meet mine as rosy lips pull into a shy smile. She's clutching her drawing pad to her chest. I told the class to draw clouds today. Partly because grades are due, partly because I need their backs turned, in case I get emotionally impaled on a Facebook picture when I send their parents invitations to the spring program.

"Ms. Abby?" In a southern school there would be no issue with the students calling me this. It shows respect, but in the north it's super weird. I can't remember when I changed it, when I asked the first student to stop calling me Ms. Sabba and use my first name instead. The months have blurred into years, but a bleeding heart doesn't recognize time. The only way I know it's passing is when report cards are due or summer is looming, like now. I dread those months of nothing to do, of being assaulted by memories that I can't control.

I glance up at Aleigha, glad to look away from the laptop for a moment. I tuck a strand of dark hair behind my ear. It wasn't out of place. "Yes, what can I help you with?"

"I was wondering what you thought of this—" Her gaze cuts to the side mid-sentence and I know she's nervous about whatever is on her sketchpad.

I reach out for her drawing pad and when I look down at the creamy paper, I'm surprised. There's a page of clouds, but instead of pencil lines and strokes each ball of mist is made of a string of zeros and ones. It looks like computer coding, all strings of numbers that mean something to techies, but not me.

I take a wild guess, "Is this binary?"

She ducks her head, hiding her face behind a wall of hair. "Not really. Well, maybe a little. I was thinking how cool it would be if the clouds could be drawn as molecules, but I didn't have my science textbook with me, so I switched to coding. Is it dumb?" Her face scrunches as uncertainty floods her features.

The one thing the girl lacks is confidence. No one ever told her that she was any good, so she's the last person to see it when she succeeds.

"This is amazing." I grasp her notepad between my hands and stare at it. The composition and flow are perfect. The fact that she did it with numbers and shading is even more entrancing. I tip the sketchpad sideways and tilt my head, admiring her work. "I don't know that much about coding. Do you?" I glance up at her.

Aleigha shakes her head. "Not really. I saw my brother messing around with something yesterday and I thought it might look cool. Robot clouds." She offers me an uncertain lopsided grin.

I hand her back her sketchpad. "You are amazing at conceptual execution. You remained true to the subject matter while infusing it with something different." Smiling softly, I add, "It feels like geo warning."

Her face lights up. "It does?"

"Yes, is that what you were hoping to achieve?" Aleigha nods fervently. "Well, go finish it up before the bell rings. You're onto something." She represses a grin as she crosses the room to peer out the window once more.

When she's settled on her stool once more with her back toward me and eyes fixed on the clouds, I return to gathering my guts to make the Facebook parent post. It's now or never. All eyes are on the sky and nowhere near me.

Ignore the pictures. Don't click around. Get away from this wall of pictures that was my life. I need to go and click the school's event page. Post, and get out. Get off of Facebook.

You'd be surprised how many clicks it takes to get to the place I need to post. Log on. Click to the school. Click the art department. And finally click on POST AN

EVENT. Swallowing hard, I manage to click my way straight to the school's page this time, into the year-end events, and I start typing, entering the information for the High School Spring Art Program. Time, directions, dates, awards, and a little graphic. I save it and close the event window.

My newsfeed reappears, because I didn't close the window, leave Facebook and walk away. It reveals a different life, someone I no longer know, but it's littered with current trending topics, like Constance Ferro running for governor of New York. But Facebook doesn't work if you don't feed it. It wants posts and ads. I've starved my account.

Since there's nothing new, old images and posts fill my cyber wall. The page is filled with ancient heartaches—Zara's smiling face looks out at me with her sun-kissed arm draped over my shoulder. The photograph was taken nearly fourteen years ago. She was closer than any friend could be and was a sister in every way, even before Zach and I got married. She was my maid of honor at our wedding. She should have been laughing, walking up and down these hallways with me now.

I scroll down. I can't help it. Social media is a black hole. Getting near the edge is enough to get sucked in for hours. Pictures I've seen before fill the glowing frame on my laptop screen and I drink them in greedily. The emotion of past moments, the echoes of laughter long silenced fill my mind.

I should stop. No one ever walked forward while constantly looking back. It's the reason I can't seem to move on with my life. The reason for the unending nightmares and a general lack of sleep. Maybe so. Or maybe I'm just angry. Zach said we'd work it out, that he wouldn't leave me—but he left me. It's not the same, but it is. Either way, I didn't want things to go this way. I'm a forty-year-old New Yorker, living on Long Island, alone. Empty house. Empty heart. Empty life.

I sigh and rest my finger on the down button, watching the promises of a former lifetime of happiness scroll by in a blur. When I blink, the page refreshes, and a new image is at the top. I'm staring at the screen, thinking I'm seeing a picture from a long time ago. There's nothing new on this account. I abandoned it when Zach died. No new pictures have been posted since. No new posts on my personal wall. Nothing.

But in this picture, Zach stands there on the beach. His beautifully ripped chest coupled with chiseled abs have more definition than I recall. He's wearing nothing but faded floral boardshorts and a crooked grin. That long, lean body stands in the sandy surf on Grand Cayman Island, on the East End somewhere, Cayman Kai, maybe? There are no tourists traps around. Just tons of turquoise water and a sandy shore leading to an old dock with a little boat.

I stare at the image. What is this? A picture from our second honeymoon? Every inch of his shirtless body is sun-kissed. A bronzed god. When he hit forty, the man began working harder to maintain his health. He started running, lifting weights, but the alcohol thickened his mid-section. I've never seen him so trim, so sculpted as he is in this photo. This picture had to be from then.

Maybe I'm not remembering right? But the man had love-handles, and this guy doesn't have an inch of fat on him. His dark hair ruffles in the wind, obscuring his face as he bends forward and ties a boat to the dock. That pose defines every muscle in his body. I can see each place I used to touch gently and trace with my fingertips. Kiss with my lips.

The dread hollowing the center of my chest fades as curiosity rises. Where were we? I must have taken this picture, but I don't remember. We were supposed to go out on a dive boat one day, but that's not the vessel. And that's not that dock we went to that day. The long wooden wharf in this picture is weather worn and old. Splintering in patches and sun-bleached. The place on Seven Mile Beach where we were supposed to depart to go diving had silver-colored aluminum planks, almost blinding in the sun. This image was taken elsewhere.

I click on the picture and make it larger. Zach is bent forward, his eyes partly hidden by the tips of his dark hair as he bends over to grab the rope. That's when I see it. The shiny spot on his torso. I double click, enlarging the image as big as it can go, thinking its sunscreen—assuming I took this picture but can't remember—or anything that is remotely logical and describes what I'm seeing because this is wrong. As my eyes sweep the light patch of skin, I instinctively know.

CHAPTER 5

*H*ands shaking, I jerk away from the computer, toppling it to the floor. Eyes wide, my skin flushes as I stagger backwards, reaching for the wall, the counter, anything so my body doesn't crash to the floor. Gaping, my mouth opens wide trying to suck in air, but it feels as if my face is covered in plastic wrap. I can't breathe.

It's not possible.

Aleigha is there, her fingers on my desk. There's a silver ring with a blood-red stone surrounded by an intricate pattern. It's the only bit of jewelry she wears. Then I realize she's repeating the same few words, "Are you all right? Should I call for help?" When I don't answer, she places her cold fingers on my arm. Her dark eyes meet mine.

A nervous laugh escapes my lips and I shake my head. Color returns to my face as my heart resumes a less frantic pace. I pat her hand and pull away. "I'm fine."

"Are you sure?" She doesn't believe me.

"Yeah," offering a fake smile, I come up with a fast explanation that sounds possible. "There was a spider on my desk. I didn't see it until it crawled onto the keyboard." OK, the story doesn't make sense, but it's enough to explain why I threw my laptop across the floor. Maybe. If she was two years old.

Aleigha's face scrunches up as she wrings her fingers. "I hate spiders." She says the words like she wants to believe me.

The entire class is watching the exchange. Every set of eyes turned from their sketchbooks, watching their teacher go insane.

Act normal. Another high-pitched plastic laugh escapes my lips. I shiver again and rub my palms over my arms. "Me too. I was so enthralled in what I was doing that it crawled across my hand. I didn't see it. When I jerked away, my laptop went flying." I glance around the room and give a girlish shrug. A few male students laugh it off, but Aleigha knows I'm lying.

She doesn't press me. Instead she picks up my computer off the floor. The screen is intact, but it's gone dark. "Let me see if I can reboot this for you. It's possible the fall broke something. Do you have a solid state hard-drive?"

I shrug, unable to find my voice. As she begins reviving the computer, the bell rings.

I repress all emotion, shoot up my stone walls around my heart in a blink, and bark out reminders for their parents to check Facebook for the invite to their Spring art show. "End of year awards will be given. And food!"

"They're already gone." Vi Trinka rounds the door. I hear the clink of her heels before I see her face. She hurries over to me. She's about my age and considers herself a catch. Plastic boobs, a trim waist, a bit of Botox in the right places, and silky black hair make it difficult to tell her exact age. But I know we're both forty years old. Tight fitting clothing hugs her thin Italian frame, an oxymoron since she loves to eat, but loves showing off that narrow waist.

We're supposed to have lunch. The woman has a sixth sense and can tell something's wrong. "What happened here? Nonni Spingoli is like screaming in my ear that something is batshit crazy right now."

Nonni is her great grandmother who came over from Italy in the early 1900's. Vi never met her but swears the woman haunts her, tells her things. Nonni's first appearance coincides with the accident. Vi was driving and Zara was on the passenger side. The right side of the car was decimated. Zara died instantly. Vi survived with a few stitches and a lot of heartache, which she combats with men and being haunted by Nonni.

Waving a hand at her, I say, "Nonni is off today. I'm just clumsy and dropped it." I lie and offer a sheepish smile.

Vi glances at my student, but Aleigha says nothing. The girl continues trying to reboot the computer.

"Nonni is never wrong." Vi arches a dark brow at me, but I offer nothing. Then she tips her head toward the door. "I'll meet you downstairs in the cafeteria, then? I don't have much time today. I need to finish grades and all the end of year shit—" she glances at student and corrects herself "—year end assignments, and so on. Let's go out tonight. Catch up." Vi wanders out, talking over her shoulder in a thick Brooklyn accent, "I won't take no for an answer."

Aleigha has the computer half alive but it sounds like it ate rocks. She frowns. "I think you're going to need a new hard drive. It wasn't solid-state so it didn't survive the crash very well. This sounds bad, but you should be able to get your stuff off of it before it totally croaks."

Without realizing it, I'm rubbing my palms over my forearms, which are covered in goosebumps with every hair standing on end. "Well, thanks for trying. I'm too clumsy sometimes."

My lips press together in a thin line. It's all over my face. Please leave. Please don't ask me. I think it so loudly that a wombat in Australia could hear me.

Aleigha notices the movement, the way my body language closed off suddenly. She tactfully ignores it. Shrugs. Accepts the way of the wombat. Tentatively, her lips move into a feint grin, and then she lies, "Yeah, me too." Then sincerely, "Hey, if you ever need help with something technical, just ask."

A nervous bark of a laugh tumbles out of my mouth. I sound like a man. Embarrassed, I find myself with my arms folded over my chest, half avoiding her gaze. "What makes you say that?"

She gives me a look that's kind, soft. "Between the time of year, Facebook, and the look on your face, Ms. Abby, it doesn't take a genius to realize something's bothering you."

I swat a hand at her as if it were nothing. All the students know my husband died suddenly on our second honeymoon and due to particularly poor form on my part, they knew we were racing towards a divorce from when I flipped out on Zach at the art show that year. Then, the unthinkable happened. We both left for vacation but only I came home. The students had a sub for six months.

I haven't personally said anything about it to them. Every time I tried, I couldn't find it in me to explain how my high school sweetheart hated me at the end, how he died—why he didn't come home—and how I got this scar across my face. Cheek to chin, a nefarious razor line, from a deep gash.

I hear them say, 'She was pretty once, before that happened.'

They speculate, say we had a huge fight—and that's when I stop listening. Lies that contain a bit of truth are the hardest to hear.

CHAPTER 6

"*I*t didn't bother me. There was a —" I'm about to say 'spider' but the girl's face makes me tell the truth. I don't want to lie to her. She's been kind to me, never took advantage of my bereavement. Even when I stupidly showed up for work and couldn't do more than sit there.

I change what I'm saying with a sigh, "Listen, I saw a picture of Zach that I don't remember taking. That's all. I wish I could remember." I need to remember, because that can't be a new shot. That makes no sense.

"There's a way to pull EXIF data from a picture, you know. If you can't remember where it was taken, or when." She speaks like this is common knowledge. Maybe it is to her, but it's not to me.

Jaw gaping, I smile politely. "Exit data?"

Aleigha shakes her head, making her dark hair tumble over her shoulders. She shoves it away like it's annoying. "EX-IF," she over-enunciates the IF at the end of the word, "data is like metadata that's stored in the photograph. Digital images have a file hidden in the actual picture. It tells you a bunch of information like what kind of camera took the picture, the exposure, lens, aperture, location, date, and a bunch of other stuff."

"Oh," I kind of want to ask her about it, but decide it's inappropriate to ask her to help me figure out when and where the picture was taken. Okay, I'm lying. I'd totally ask her, but I don't want her asking questions about Zach, about my scar, or what happened.

"I can pull it for you," she offers. "I watch this guy on YouTube. He's a pro photographer and he talks about this at length in one of his videos. I wouldn't mind helping you pull it"

"Thanks, but I'll just look up how to do it.

It's personal, but thank you. I didn't realize there was that much information in an image." I sound like my mother. Technology passed me by, and I didn't even notice. Exit data. Geeze.

"There is, unless someone stripped it. Like I said, YouTube. Search for Cole's Camera Class and you'll find the video." She beams at me. "I'm off to lunch. If you change your mind, just ask." Aleigha gathers her things and is out the door.

As soon as I'm alone, my heart starts slamming into my chest hard enough to bruise a lung. I know what I saw. It was him. I'm left feeling shaken, with a thin sheen of sweat on my skin that has nothing to do with the balmy spring air. It scares me. I barely made it through Zara's death, then when Zach died—my God.

My hand is touching the thin scar that divides my right cheek into two planes. Separated by a single event. The pads of my fingers trace the thin line as I stare, unseeing at the cinderblock walls. There's no pale-yellow paint. No flickering fluorescents above. Time stops and turns back. I'm there in Grand Cayman, smiling. Feeling so angry, spitting the words at him in the dive shop. I hate you. Zach storms off, planning to dive without me, and disappears into the back room to get his gear. Then, an ear-piercing crack rumbles me to my core, causing me to turn toward the sound. That horrifying noise. I sway on my feet.

Then, nothing.

No sound.

No sight.

Just a cloud of unbreathable ash, searing my lungs. And the mirror that hung on the wall, the one I'd been looking into, bursts. It fractures before I can blink, splintering into an array of flashing, flying shards. A metal support beam crashes behind me, shaking the floor and making chunks of concrete go airborne. If I didn't turn toward the sound of the explosion, I'd be dead. Instead, I'm left breathing with an angry scar on my face.

Swallowing hard, I force my hand down. Breathe. Blink. Stop this foolishness. He's gone. They're both dead. I chide myself and try to shake the shiver that's kissed my skin, but I can't. No matter how much I want to say that was Zach—that he's alive and I saw him in a picture today—logically I know it's not possible. I'd write it off to a Facebook glitch. That makes the most sense, but there's one glaring problem.

I've never seen that photo before.

CHAPTER 7

*V*i sits across the table from me. The dark lacquered top reflects her beautiful face. Exotic. She was the hot one, I was the hippie, and Zara was country with a K. I'm not talking superficial, like women that start saying *ya'll* and wear overalls. She was everything I'm not. There was a wildness in her soul that couldn't be tamed.

We were a good balance, the three of us. I anchored Zara. Vi widened my worldviews and made the exotic appealing. Made me see how I could be so much more. And Zara gave me the courage to chase freedom. To actually have the guts to not only dream, but reach out and grab it. She had a way of making anything sound possible.

When she died, I battened the hatches, leaned hard on Zach, and waited for the hollowness in my chest to fade. When he died, I don't know what became of me. The woman sitting in a bar on a school night is not the woman he married. It's not Zara's old roommate either.

Vi stares at me with those piercing dark eyes. Her hair is expanding with the evening humidity. The door to the bar is open to the street. There's a steady hum of cars and evening air cooling the place. Some people might call it a dive, but I love it. Vi found it a few months back.

The exterior is unassuming on main street in Huntington Village. The AC is dead or never was. The light fixtures cast an amber glow. A few fixtures are original, dating back a hundred years. The bar is from the same era—the roaring 20's. Its massive mahogany wood is gleaming, set across the room from us. There's a spattering of tiny cast iron tables with velvet tufted seats that surround the bar with matching cheater booths lining the walls. Curtains and all. A blue and white art deco tiled floor is original and runs right up to the brass footrest that lines the wooden bar.

Three local guys with white t-shirts clinging to their skin wear vintage high waisted pants and play live music from the era, mostly jazz. It's strange, what a couple of brass players and a bass can do. The place hums. It's as if it's alive, breathing across the century, telling the tale of women who came before me. Sat in my seat. Got hammered by life. And lived on.

The music makes my body sway. Or maybe that's the drink. Jack. Ice. Nothing fancy. I've been holding the whiskey glass halfway to my lips and staring at the trumpet player. He's got dark hair that's slicked back with sweat. His shirt clings to his body as he plays, eyes closed, his body moving to the music.

There are couples pressed together on the dance floor, moving their feet in sync with the music—doing dances that are beyond me. There's one couple, a guy with a familiar face with dark hair that he keeps pushing out of his eyes. His piercing blue gaze sparkles when it meets his dance partner's. Her long curls swirl as he whips her around and then yanks her back, quickly. If it wasn't this dive, I'd swear that was one of the Ferro guys. The older two look alike. I'd think they were twins if I didn't know better. But this can't be him. Why would he be here in this dive?

Vi's thick accent finally cuts through my thick thoughts of the rich and famous when her pointy toed stiletto meets my shin. "Hello-o. I'm talking to you." Her dark brows shoot up her face impatiently. "I know something rattled you today. Talk." That word sounds like it has a few W's in it. *Tawwk.*

Sighing, I place the glass on the table. My eyes shift between the musician and Vi. "There's nothing to talk about."

"Bull. Shit." Her red nails gleam in the dim light. She's always polished. Looks perfect on the outside. Inside is a hot mess. Not that I'm judging, because I'm not. She was in the car with Zara when she died. Vi blames herself even though it wasn't her fault. At all.

"Seriously. It's nothing. The same old

crap. I had to post the Spring event. I scrolled."

Her eyes grow large. This isn't the first time I looked at Facebook since the funeral, but every time I do it results in days of tears and an emotional tidal wave that crushes me flat. Vi spits out, "You didn't."

"I did." Except I'm not flat this time. I'm still upright and breathing in a bar. "And it's still the same. Everyone is still dead. I'm here. You're here. I'm a bitch. You're crazy. And that sums things up." I'm lifting my glass to my lips when she snatches it away.

She snaps her long-tapered fingers at the waiter. "Coffee, please. Now." She redirects her gaze at me. "You've got to pull yourself together."

I snort. "Look who's talking. You think you can see ghosts."

She stiffens, her spine going ramrod straight. "I can. And since when did you get all judgey?"

The waiter places a white coffee cup in front of me and fills it with steaming black liquid. The scent hits me hard. Memories of lost laughter bounce inside my skull. When we were in college, the three of us would stay up all night, drinking coffee at this little shop that was on a street in the Village. It's gone now, but the memories remain. They cling to life no matter how hard I try to let the past die.

Disgusted, I push it away. "I'm not. It's just that—" I break off. It's not the lump in my throat, because it's not there. I feel dead inside. It shocks me that the music can penetrate my mood. That I feel the rhythmic hum despite myself.

Vi tilts her head to the side. "It's just that what?"

"Years have passed. I feel like my entire life has ghosted out. It's not there anymore, but I'm still here." I'm staring at the mirror behind the bar while I speak, unable to meet her gaze. "Still here, but not."

"Out of all people, don't you think I know how that feels? I lost them too."

My gaze flicks to hers. It's mean, but I say it anyway, "He wasn't your husband. I don't even know if he was mine. That trip. It was so last second. It felt, I don't know. I shouldn't have pushed him to do something. Zara was fate, but Zach was on me."

Vi chokes, slams her glass down, and gets this possessed look in her eye. "That was not your fault."

"Everyone said it was." I reach for my glass of whiskey and she doesn't stop me. "It's that time of year again, which means the story is going to run."

"Jesus Christ, is that what has you twisted up?" Her anger turns, juts out at press that aren't here. "They're bullshit stories from hack reporters. Besides! No one believes that."

The newspapers say I killed Zach. They present a different angle each year. Once they even had proof of the murder weapon that I'd tossed into the sea. I murmur, "My students see it. They call me—"

"I know what they call you. I work there too. Have you heard what they say about me?" She presses her hand to her chest before flicking her wrist away from her body, fingers spread wide with irritation. "Fuck it. I can't talk to you when you're like this." She stands, opens her purse and digs a few bills out. Throws them on the table.

The urge to tell her about the picture overwhelms me. It's the reason for my foul mood. The reason why I don't want to go home. It's too hard not to sit down in front of the computer and look for it. "Vi, wait."

CHAPTER 8

I place my hand on her wrist. Her eyes flick to the touch.

"What?" she snaps at me and has every right to. I'm being a bitch.

"I saw him. A picture." The words choke me, and I can't make them come out. Growling, I down the rest of my drink, slam the glass on the table, and manage, "There was a scar on his side. But it was Zach."

Vi's brow creases. She sits down hard. "Wait. What are you saying? That it's a new picture?" There's no judgement in her tone. I don't meet her gaze. I can't. So, I shrug. Instead of dismissing it, she lets the information sink in, then asks, "Where? Facebook?"

ALL THE BROKEN PIECES

"Yeah." I pull the cup of coffee in front of me and slide my index finger across the smooth porcelain handle. "It popped up. Freaked me out. And now... I don't know. The image was only there for a second. I'm wrong. It had to be from our trip—"

"Why do you say that?"

"Because it was the Caribbean. The color of the water and the sky. It wasn't here. But it wasn't from our trip."

"So, what are you thinking? That he had another life in the Caribbean and social media decided to show you. Now?" Neither of us says anything for a moment. Then she adds, "It can't be from now. You buried him. It's the main reason his mother hates your guts."

"That's an understatement. But yeah, I know. So, if it's not from now, when was it taken? I want to see it again, but I don't. I can't go home, Vi." My face falls, shatters. I wish I could cry but my tears dried up a long time ago. "I can't deal with all of this."

Vi's head jerks back and she lifts a finger. "The reporters will be shot if they step on your lawn. I promise you that. Okay."

"You can't promise that."

"The hell, I can't!" she leans forward. "I've got connections. They'll stay away. Some asshole might run the story recap, but it'll be buried if they have no pictures. See what I'm sayin'?"

"Yeah." My voice sounds hollow. Half alive.

"As for the rest of it. Wait. I'll watch Facebook for pictures of him. You don't have to do that."

I want to pull my hair out, so I feel something. Anything besides pain. "What for? To confirm he went off without me? Vi, if he was cheating on me... I can't. I don't want to know."

Vi taps a red nail in the center of the table. "If you're holding onto that guy and he was an asshole, disappearing in the middle of the night—"

"That only happened once."

"You only caught him once. I don't want to be a bitch about this, but oh-my-effen-God! After Zara died, he lost it. It wasn't your fault."

My voice shrinks and I feel so small that it

barely comes out. "I don't remember him like that."

"I know you don't, but it's time to remember all that shady shit that was going on. Zach was up to no good. Guys that stay out all night and get caught aren't good guys. You forgave before you even found out what happened. Don't you want to know the truth?" Vi reaches out and touches my hand. Rests hers on top.

I pull away. Indifference fills me from head to toe. "I'm so tired of this. I just don't want this life anymore. Vi…" my voice cracks and I hate myself for it.

"So, make a new one."

"If only it were that easy."

Vi tips back the rest of her drink, then agrees, "If only. Two hot high school teachers take over the town."

I didn't realize the music stopped until I glance at the man standing behind Vi. His hair has a bit of a curl to it, dark and tousled. There's a trace of stubble on lining his jaw and if that t-shirt clings any tighter, it would be skin. "Which town would that be?"

Vi grins, twists in her seat and her face

goes neutral before she says, silky smooth—
not horrified in the least— "eavesdropping
isn't sexy. Move along." She waves him off
and turns back towards me.

I try not to laugh. The guy doesn't walk
away. There are women drooling at him from
across the room, and the one he tried to talk
to blew him off. He grabs a chair from
another table, flips it around, and straddles it
before asking Vi, "Then tell me what is sexy,
because I hear that two hot high school
teachers are about to do some amazing
things." He winks at me before returning his
burning gaze toward Vi.

Before the flirting goes any further, I
stand and grab my purse. "Not this one. I've
got to get home."

He looks me over, and it's clearly to make
Vi jealous, and says, "Too bad. And then there
was one." He turns his gaze on Vi as he says
the last word. The tension is as thick as the
night air.

Vi laughs and stands with me. "Yeah, you."

Smiling, I point at her. "Sit. Talk. Ask him
how hard he blows that thing." I'm referring

to the trumpet, but her face turns as red as her nails.

The musician represses a grin, looks up at Vi, "Ask me."

Vi giggles. She slowly sits as I walk over to the bar and pay our tab. There's a small painting on the wall by a local guy—Jack Gray. I gesture to the canvas, because it's out of place here. And I'm a fan. "How'd you come across that piece?"

The barkeep is a college girl, golden hair pulled up into a high ponytail, face full of expertly applied make-up. "It's the owners."

"Really?" I look around again. I guess if I can appreciate the artistry of this place, why not?

"Yes, he bought it out a few years back. There's another one in Port Jeff."

I nod, taking my change and stuffing some cash in the tip jar, before wishing her a good night.

When I glance back at our table, Vi and the musician talking, inching closer so that they're nose to nose by the time I leave. At least one of us will have a good night.

CHAPTER 9

The night blurs into every other night. Just as every day goes on without end bleeding into the next with little differentiation. The hole in my chest consumes me. Grief swallowed everything and spit out my bones. All I can do is keep breathing and get to the next day. At some point it should get easier, but not now. Not tonight.

Emotions are sloshing in my chest like a kid carrying a fish tank. They splash out and ruin everything I touch. I have no idea why Vi puts up with me. She's handling it better than me, but she didn't lose her husband.

Sitting on the edge of my bed, I rub my eyes with the heel of my hand. Assuming Zach was cheating is horrible, but he was doing something. My senses knew it then and I know it now. Digging around in his past won't help me move forward, so I don't. Instead, I think about the happy times. It's the only way the pressure on my chest eases. I can breathe if I remember him. His beautiful smile. The dimple on his cheek. The way his cheeks felt between my palms when I kissed his lips. The roughness of the stubble lining his jaw. The dark hair that fell into those blue eyes. The way his lips tugged up at the corners ever so slightly when he teased me. The vacant gaze and plastic pleasantries towards the end. The way we sat in the same room and silence swallowed us whole. That trip was supposed to help us reconnect. Work got between us. Life knocked us down. I thought he'd still be here. Instead, I'm alone wondering if he was an asshole. Wondering if I knew him at all.

"Ahhhh," I grumble in the back of my throat, letting the sound rip out like a wounded animal. "What the hell is wrong with me?" I say it to no one. Sighing, I glance into the long mirror on the wall opposite the bed. It's tilted against the wall, reflecting me. Here. Alone. "I need to get a dog and stop talking to myself."

The night passes slowly. I lay in bed staring at the ceiling, thinking about nothing and everything all at once. Every part of my soul was stripped bare. This raw feeling consumes me to the point that I don't trust my instincts anymore.

The crisp white sheets cling to my skin in the balmy night. I twist and turn, and finally doze off thinking about Zach. My mind moves in slow circles until it lands gently on a pleasant memory—our honeymoon in Paris. Our love lock, placed on a bridge. Newlyweds and completely in love, we spent every moment tangled together. The way he looked at me made me feel alive. His gaze lit my body on fire. I was pliant in his arms as he traced every inch of me with his fingers and then covered me in kisses. The lacey lingerie and the posh room at the Ritz with a chandelier hanging over a fluffy bed with a white coverlet. We never left the room. I can still feel the way he moved against me. I still see his eyes, feel the warmth of his breath as he pressed his lips to my skin again and again, showering me in affection. My body curved into his. It was like he was made for me. The way we intertwined, slick with sweat and breathing hard, was unlike anything I'd ever imagined. Then, after we were spent, he wrapped his sculpted arms around me.

His finger traces the curls clinging to my cheek. His voice is deep, still filled with desire. "My beautiful wife."

He rolls the word around in his mouth and kisses my temple. My body curves against his, my bare hips nestled against his as he trails his lips over my neck. After he slides his tongue along the outside curve of my ear, he rests his hand on my breast.

Sated and sleepy, he whispers, "My wife, my Greek goddess. I love you Abbey."

With those strong hands on my body and the way he watched me back then, I felt like a goodness when I was with him. It was impossible not to in those early years. Men like that are in fairytales. I had one and I lost him. If I'm being honest with myself, I lost him long before I buried him in the ground.

CHAPTER 10

The window is open, and a white curtain with lacy trim billows at the edge of the sill. It's a warm night. The scent of jasmine sweeps into the bedroom. I'm tangled in the sheets, laying on my back, straining to hear the noise again. Downstairs. There was a sound. I'm so tired and emotionally spent. Do I care if I get robbed?

My eyelids are heavy and weariness clings to my sweaty skin. Emptiness fills the house. The sounds of floorboards settling and creaking have fallen silent. I shift in my bed, shoving the covers between my legs, and then flatten my pillow. No one is downstairs, but the hairs on my arms raise. I can't get the sinking feeling out of the pit of my stomach. The house, this little cape, is empty. I'm the only one here, but—crap. I can't leave it alone. I can't act like I didn't hear it. Or maybe I can. It's the middle of the night.

Groaning unladylike expletives, I shove my face into my pillow and lay there, face-down. I count, listening. One. Two. The truth is, after all this time, my heart still jumps into high gear if I hear the faintest sound. Like it's doing now. Three. Four. Five. As if the accident just happened. It didn't just happen. The problem is that my brain recognizes that nearly three years have passed since that horrible, godforsaken day, but my heart has no clue.

My heart plays tricks on me, making me feel a tug in one direction down a random street, past the bakery, until I see a man, tall, trim, with a dusting of dark stubble on his jaw. For a moment, I think it's him—my husband—but then he turns. It's never him. And I know why, but my heart is utterly confused, drunk with hope.

So, I shove that part of my mind into a mental closet, remove all sharp objects, and let her rant about whatever crazy crap she wants. As long as it doesn't spill into my head, my heart can have at it in the closet.

That sound. What is it? It's light, metallic almost—but not. It has to be sounds of the house settling. It makes weird noises when it's too hot or too cold.

Gripping the pillow tightly, I push it away and sigh, sitting up. I run a hand through my dark hair, shoving back the curl by my face that's turned gray. I should dye it but I'm not the salon type. Truth be told, I've lost too much weight, erasing a decent pair of hips and a nice set of tits in the process. Now I'm flat girl, coming and going. I'm Flat Stanley. It's that bad. But I can't seem to make myself care.

I tug my hair into a ponytail that sits low at the base of my neck before pulling it over my shoulder. I swear, it almost sounds like wood scraping on concrete. It's so soft, but I hear it. I glance over at the cologne still on the other nightstand. Ferro. Zach had to have that for Christmas. Sometimes I spray it on the sheets because I can't stand that his scent is gone from the house. It's been too long. So the bottle remains.

I take a huge gulp of air and wish I refilled my Xanax prescription. No one knows what I've lived through, not even the shrink. It's not a common occurrence to lose your husband and best-friend within a few months. In fact, my husband's accident was so weird, they thought I did something to cause it initially. Bastards. As if I'd blow half my face off and risk being crushed in the debris.

But still. People whisper. The fact that our relationship was strained makes those mutterings worse. The overwhelming desire to slam my fist into the reporters' faces is hard to control. I never fought back when Zach was alive. That part of me backed away. Zach always took care of things. I let him.

Now things are different. If I don't fight back, well, I wouldn't still be here. Anger fuels me, moving me through the minutes of the day. If there's a reporter downstairs, I swear I'll lose it. There's no intentionality in my life, in the person I'm becoming. But I don't care if I don't recognize the woman in the mirror anymore. Surviving is paramount. I'll figure out who I am when the dust settles. Until then, I'm lost in the fog trying to find a way out.

Suddenly there's a loud *CRACK* that carries up to my window. Glass shatters downstairs. I'm sure of it. Jumping from the bed, I pad across the room in a threadbare T shirt and knit shorts. They don't match. Before passing the closet in a rush, I reach inside and grab a wooden baseball bat that once belonged to Zach.

My feet hit the wooden steps in rapid succession, slamming down hard against the floor. One hand barely touches the railing, and I've got the bat clutched in the other. When I get to the upper landing, I glance around. Nothing. No one. Shoving my hand through my hair, I make an exasperated sound and stomp down the rest of the steps, annoyed.

Amber lights glow softly, illuminating the

base of the staircase, but the foyer is dark. I'm perched, still standing on the bottom step, hand on the banister, eyes sweeping the room. The mahogany wooden floor has a crimson glow in the moonlight. There's no tall nefarious guy in a black mask. I almost wish there was.

Gingerly lifting my leg, I place it down on the floor, and stop. That's when I feel it—a warm breeze. It tickles my ankles as it catches the tiny hairs on my unshaved legs. My spine straightens as I lift my face slowly, back toward the front door. Every hair on my body stands on end as my stomach tightens. My fingers turn white as I strangle the bat in my hand.

The front door is surrounded by glass panes, each one hand-made by an artist I found in Brooklyn. Each pane is no taller than my palm and hand-blown with the palest kiss of blue. I commissioned them when my shrink, Dr. Patel, suggested a project to help distract me from my heartache. Making over this old house seemed like a good idea when we were first married. The little cape is a block from the

ALL THE BROKEN PIECES

canal in Lindenhurst, a small hamlet on Long Island.

Zach and I always wanted to live here, close to his family, near the train, and not too far from Manhattan. We dreamed of rescuing this old house that had been boarded up since the hurricane ripped through a few years back. Back then, it'd been a dream. Now it's a lonely nightmare and I'm not entirely certain how I got here.

The scent of roses fills my head as I creep toward the door, slithering through the darkness with my heart in my throat. Someone is there, in the shadows. Squaring my shoulders, I stride swiftly toward the massive front door and shift the grip on my bat. The sheen of the black lacquer is unmarred. The antique brass door pull is still intact. There's no sign of entry. The hairs on my arms stand on end. I turn slowly, pivoting, scanning, waiting to see the intruder.

I call out into the air. "Shoot me or get the hell out. I've got work in the morning." My voice cracks, not with fear, but with annoyance.

I press my lower lip upward so tightly

that my teeth nick my skin. The gentle creaks of the old stairs re-settling are my only response. Another warm breeze licks my bare ankles before it catches the hem of my gown, making it flitter around my ankles. I glance at the door, leerily and stride toward it. My eyes fixate on a splotch of darkness where an artesian blue pane of glass once resided. Now there is only a black patch of darkness. The crunch of glass under my foot hits my ears as fragments of glass sink into my flesh. I swear under my breath and step away. Pieces of thick glass lay on the dark wooden planks, making them difficult to see until I'm on top of them.

The glass pane is shattered with shards lining the foyer floor. Someone broke one of the panes. Was this a botched break in? I think about grabbing my phone to call it in, but decide against it. A broken window could be a kid throwing rocks. That's happened before and the cops don't like coming out for that kind of thing. Zach wouldn't call if he were here, so I don't. That's when I see it. A huge, dark, hunk of metal, the size of my palm, is laying on the floor.

Before I hobble toward it, I balance awkwardly against the wall and pluck the glass from my foot. After I've gotten most of it, I gimp along on my heel, smearing a crimson trail of blood in my wake. The truth is, the pain feels good. I'll never admit it, but it's better than feeling helpless, better than crushing grief that lingers on for days on end.

Plucking the culprit from the shadows, I straighten and hold the heavy thing to the light. It's a piece of lead with a dolphin in a circle and the number 4. It's a weight from a dive belt. Rubbing my thumb over the dolphin, I feel something scratched onto the back. When I flip it over, the smooth side of the weight has been marred, the smooth surface gone. Deep gouges spell out a single word. A warning.

STOP.

READY FOR MORE? This is a FAN DRIVEN SERIES!
When you ask for more, you get more!

SO ASK IN A REVIEW & ON SOCIAL MEDIA!

* * *

THEN MAKE SURE YOU DON'T MISS IT

Text **HMWARD** (one word) to **24587** for a text reminder on release day.

COMPLETED SERIES BY
H.M. WARD

ROMANCE

~SECRETS & LIES~

~STRIPPED~

~THE PROPOSITION~

~DAMAGED~

~LIFE BEFORE DAMAGED~

~SECRETS~

~SECRET LIFE OF TRYSTAN SCOTT~

~SCANDALOUS~

TEEN PARANORMAL

~DEMON KISSED~

Please turn the page for a suggested reading order.

THE ARRANGEMENT 24

THE ARRANGEMENT 25

THE ARRANGEMENT 26

CAN'T WAIT FOR H.M. WARD'S NEXT STEAMY BOOK?

*Let her know by leaving stars and telling her
what you liked about this book in a review!*

KID READS

NEED A BOOK FOR YOUR KID?

~RISE OF THE OLYMPIANS~ (FREE)

~RISE OF THE OLYMPIANS 2~

~RISE OF THE OLYMPIANS 3~

~RISE OF THE OLYMPIANS 4~

~RISE OF THE OLYMPIANS 5~

~RISE OF THE OLYMPIANS 6~

ABOUT THE AUTHOR

New York Times bestselling author H.M. Ward continues to reign as the queen of independent publishing. She swiftly sold over 20 MILLION copies of her books worldwide, placing her among the literary titans. Articles pertaining to Ward's success have appeared in The *New York Times, USA Today,* and *Forbes* to name a few. This native New Yorker resides in Texas with her family, where she enjoys working on her next book.

You can interact with this bestselling author at:
www.hmward.com